P9-DCL-482

For Amy, Nina, Don, Cuddles + Teh-bear

Two Bear Cubs

Ann Jonas

This edition is published by special arrangement with Greenwillow Books,
a division of William Morrow & Company, Inc.

Grateful acknowledgment is made to Greenwillow Books,
a division of William Morrow & Company, Inc. for permission to reprint

Printed in the United States of America

ISBN 0-15-315203-6

2 3 4 5 6 7 8 9 10 060 02 01 00

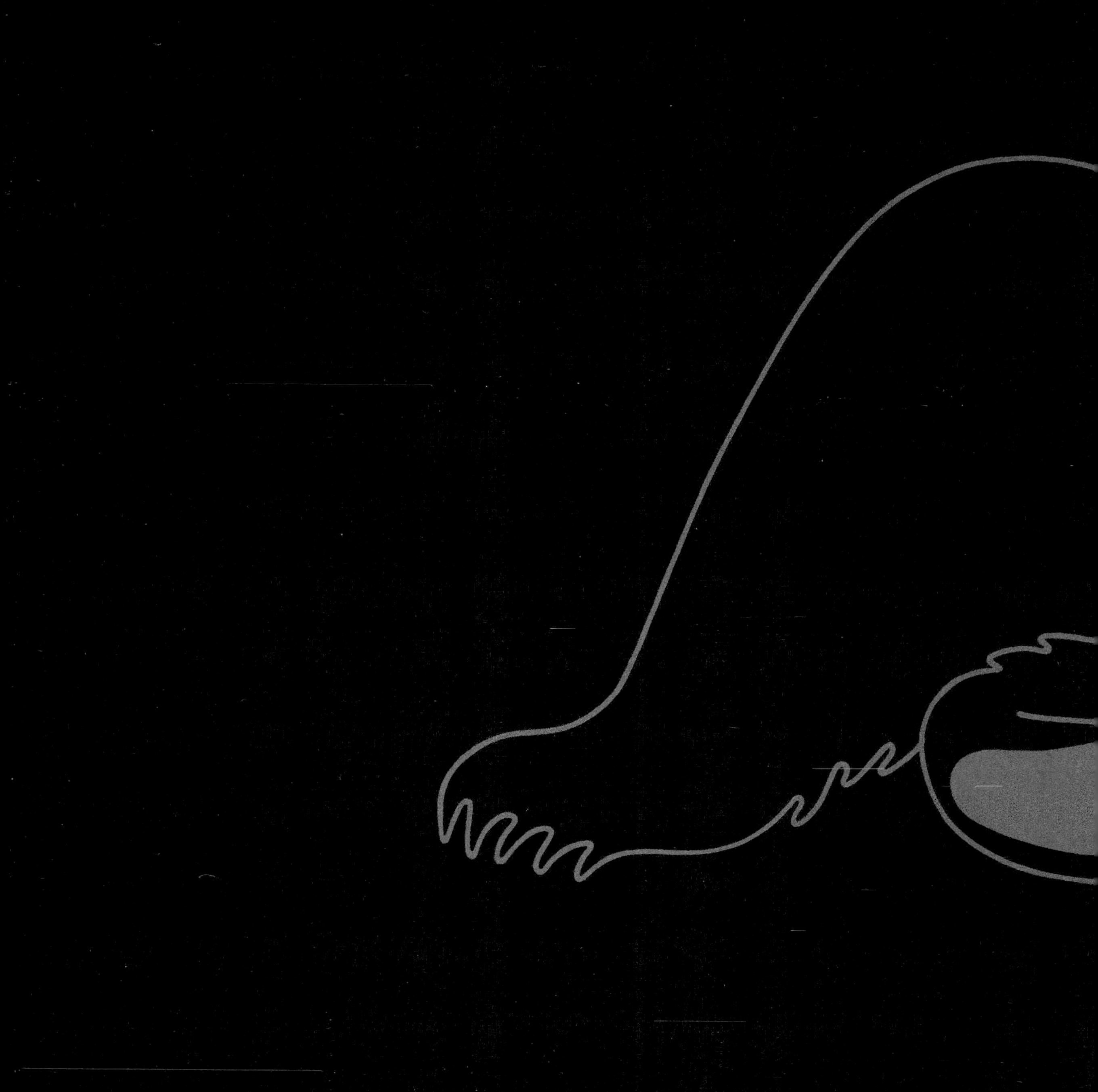

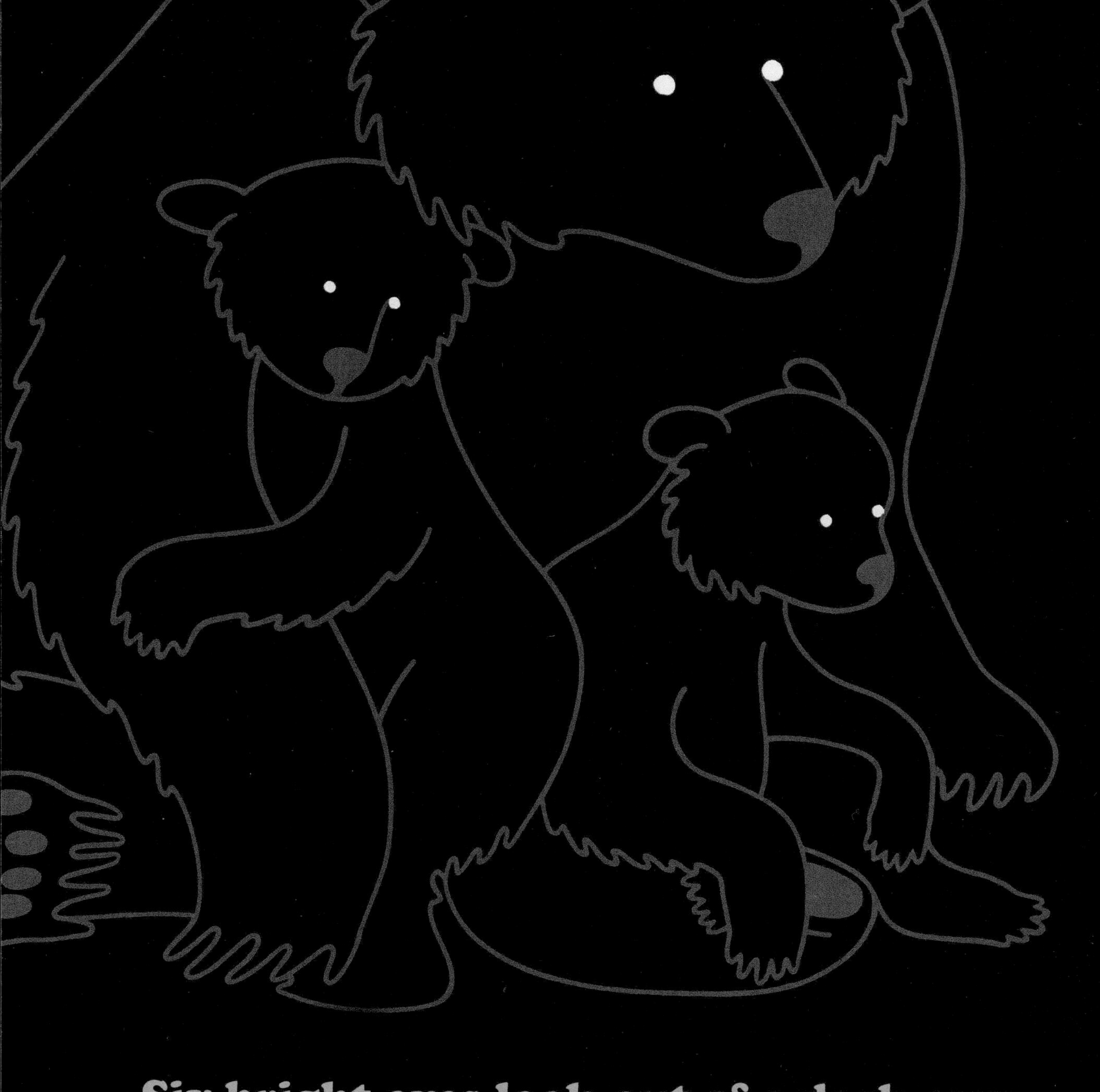

Six bright eyes look out of a dark cave.

A bear and her cubs begin their day.

The mother watches while her cubs play.

Something walks by.
It doesn't smell like a bear.

The cubs follow it.

It follows them!

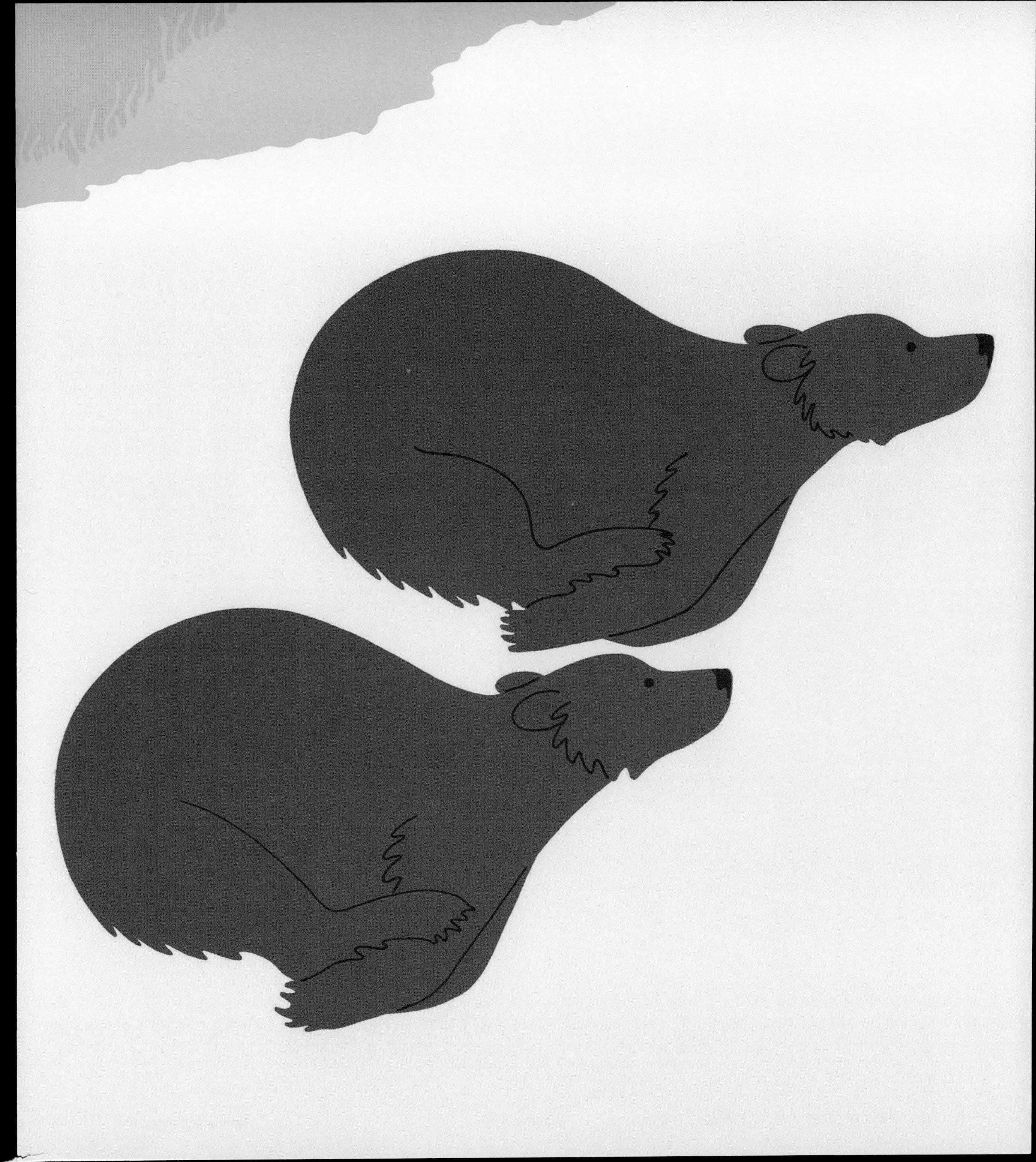

At last they outrun it.
But where are they?

And where is their mother?

They look around.
They sniff the ground.

No mother.

They find a honey tree all by themselves—

and a lot of angry bees!

Where is their mother?

They can't even catch a fish.
Where can their mother be?

There she is!

And they aren't even very far from home.